W9-CAR-868

I belong to
THE BEST BOOK CLUB EVER™
This is my book.

My name is

....

Will you please read it to me?

The Jackson Family's New Baby Boy

A Random House PICTUREBACK®

The Jackson

Granddad Parker

Granny Parker

Grandpa Jackson

Grandma Jackson

Mom

Dad

Copyright © 1978 by Random House, Inc. All rights reserved under International and Pan-American Copyright Conventions.
Published in the United States by Random House, Inc., New York, and simultaneously in Canada by Random House of Canada
Limited, Toronto. First published in Spain as *Asi Es Nuestro Hermano Pequeno* by Ediciones Altea, Madrid. © 1977 by Ediciones
Altea, Madrid. Library of Congress Catalog Card Number: 77-85679. ISBN: 0-394-83715-0 (B.C.); 0-394-84032-1 (trade).
Manufactured in the United States of America   . B C D E F G H I J   1 2 3 4 5 6 7 8 9 0

Smudge

Family's
New Baby Boy

illustrated by Ulises Wensell

Jenny

Steve

David

RANDOM HOUSE ⌂ NEW YORK

Everyone in the Jackson family was excited about the new baby boy. When Mom, Dad, and Granny Parker first brought him home from the hospital, Jenny and Steve and Granddad Parker were waiting at the door. Smudge was there too, wagging his tail.

Steve thought the baby seemed very small. But Dad said he would grow.

The whole family helped choose a name for him. Jenny and Steve liked David, and that's what he was called.

David slept most of the day. But he was often awake at night.

Mom had to give him a bottle every few hours, and Dad rocked the bassinet when David cried.

No one got much sleep.

For some reason David didn't like to take his bath.
Steve waved toys at him, and Jenny played peek-a-boo
with his towel. But David went right on screaming.
Poor Smudge just tried to hide.

As David grew bigger,
he seemed to grow happier,
though he still slept most
of the time.

Jenny and Steve always
left some of their toys near
his playpen when they went
off to school.

On weekends Granny and Granddad Parker took David to the park to give Mom and Dad a rest.

While Jenny and Steve played with their friends, David kicked happily in his carriage.

Granny Parker and Grandma Jackson made a big fuss over David. Granny said his eyes were just like Mom's. Grandma said David looked just like Dad when *he* was a baby.

When David's first teeth
began to grow in, everything
he could grab went right into
his mouth.

He even chewed on some
flowers in the plant shop.

David never seemed to get enough to eat.

One night Dad found him in a corner with a whole bunch of bananas!

Soon David began to crawl. He loved looking into mirrors, and he told himself stories that neither Jenny nor Steve could understand.

Mom said he was trying to talk. Anyway, it kept him out of mischief while Jenny and Steve were buying new shoes.

David was forever getting into mischief. He broke a lot of Jenny and Steve's toys.

Dad said he just wanted to see what was inside them.

But Jenny and Steve were furious!

Jenny and Steve were very excited when David began to walk.

At first Jenny had to help him, and Granny Parker was always nearby, ready to catch him.

But David didn't mind if he tumbled. He quickly learned to get around by himself.

After he learned to walk,
David began to climb. Now
nothing was safe!

One day he piled up some
boxes to reach a toy Santa
Claus on the Christmas tree.

Grandpa Jackson caught
him just before he fell.

David wasn't a bit afraid
of the dark. Often he got
up in the middle of the night
to find one of his toys.

Soon David was big
enough to go everywhere
the rest of the family went.
   Jenny and Steve showed
him all their favorite
animals at the zoo. David
liked the lions best.

In the summer, they all went to the beach. David loved
the water. Right away he wanted to go in swimming with
Jenny and Steve. Mom said she would have to teach him.
The Jackson family's new baby boy was no longer a baby!